For Dee, who has a heart as big as Texas. — TM

For the boys — Zane, Lukas and Noah. — TS

A TeXaS YEAR

TWELVE MONTHS IN THE LIFE OF TEXAN KIDS

TANIA MCCARTNEY + TINA SNERLING

EK

Welcome to Texas

Hello, I'm MIA. I'm 6 and I love cooking and horseback riding. My mom is American and my dad is from Argentina. When I'm older, I want to be a mom and a Tex-Mex chef.

Annyeong! My name is CHRISTOPHER and I'm 8 years old. My dad was born in Texas and my mom is from Korea. I love computer games. One day, I'd like to be a computer scientist.

Hi y'all! I'm ALEXIS and I love animals and pageants. I'm 9 years old and I'm a champion line dancer. When I grow up, I want to be Miss America.

Howdy, I'm ETHAN--the biggest Houston Texans fan ever. I'm 7 and I love drawing and playing the guitar. When I'm grown, I want to be a rock star or a paleontologist.

Hola! I'm LUIS and I'm 10. I was born in Mexico and came to Texas when I was 3. I grew up with horses and one day I want to ride in rodeos and play baseball for the Texas Rangers.

JANUARY

January is one of our COLDEST months.

1ST

It's NEW YEAR'S DAY! We eat black-eyed peas and wear something new.

On the WEEKEND, we have sleepovers, go horseback riding or ride our bikes.

BLACK-EYED PEAS

SQUEAK!

CHIPS

CRACKERS

CHIPS

COOKIES

CANDY

PRETZELS

We have lots of favorite SNACKS.

We have TEA PARTIES with our hamsters.

Our golden retrievers love RUNNING in the park.

We keep busy after SCHOOL.

YEEHAW!

HOMEWORK

COMPUTER GAMES

TRAMPOLINE

TEJAS means "friends."

Sometimes, SNOW falls in the north of Texas.

Grandpa loves his COWBOY HAT.

Martin Luther King, Jr. DAY

20TH

EVERY FOUR YEARS

It's INAUGURATION Day.

February

On GROUNDHOG DAY, we learn when Spring will arrive.

2ND

MOO!

MARDI GRAS MEANS "FAT TUESDAY."

We go to the local RODEO to see some bull riding, barrel racing, and roping. The pig races are fun.

IT'S GEORGE WASHINGTON'S BIRTHDAY!

It's MARDI GRAS! We catch strings of beads as the parade moves through town.

TEDDY BEAR

CARDS

CANDY

14TH

PRESIDENT'S DAY

On VALENTINE'S DAY, we might get a card from a secret admirer.

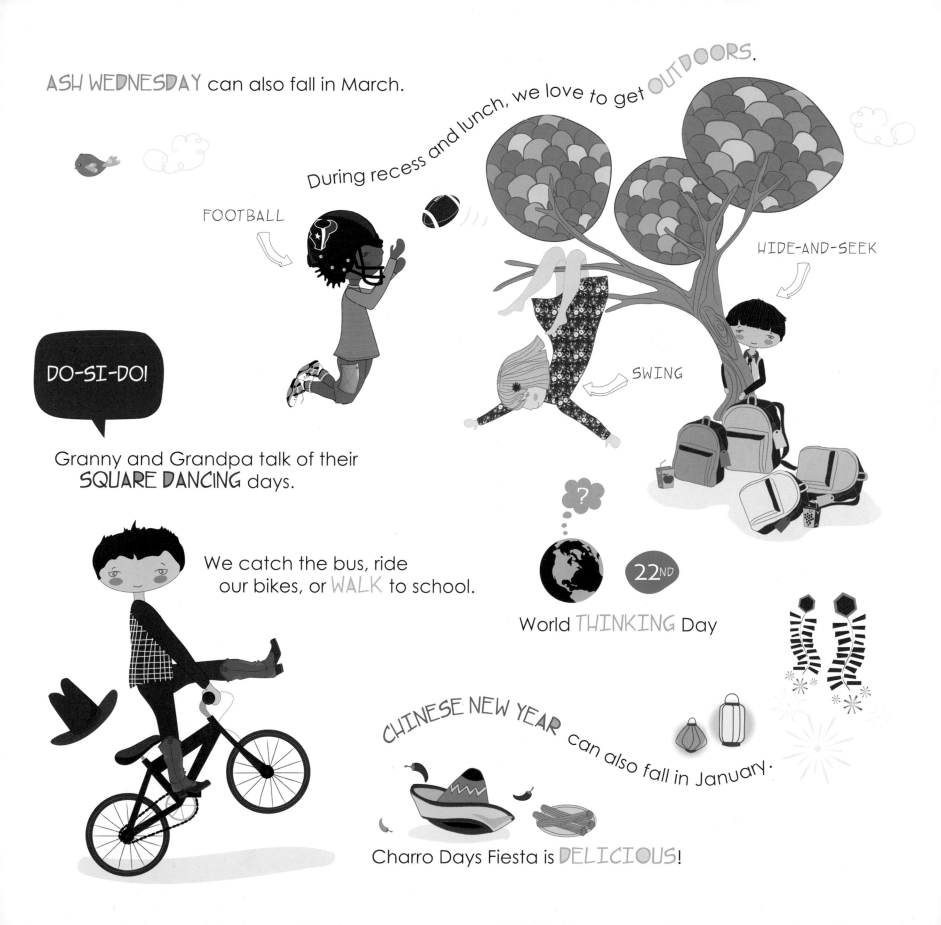

March

It's SPRING! It's also the start of the tornado season in Texas.

2ND
It's Texas INDEPENDENCE Day!

2ND
On Dr. Seuss's birthday, we haul out BOOKS for Read Across America Day.

CHILI CON CARNE

CHEESE ENCHILADAS

TACOS

QUESO DIP

FAJITAS

We just love TEX-MEX food.

DAYLIGHT SAVING begins. Clocks go forward one hour.

It's Spring Break. We have a WEEK off school!

On ST. PATRICK'S DAY, everything is green!

17ᵀᴴ

We go CAMPING in the Prairies and Lakes region.

TENT

COYOTES HOWLING

CAMPFIRE

FLASHLIGHT

S'MORES

It's RATTLESNAKE Roundup in Sweetwater.

BLUEBONNETS start to pop.
They paint the hillsides blue.

31ˢᵀ

CÉSAR CHÁVEZ Day

Sometimes, EASTER falls in March.

I LOVE BEING A KID!

The Houston CHILDREN'S FESTIVAL begins.

April

It's April FOOLS' Day.
Mom short-sheets our beds!

It's PASSOVER.

GO TEXAS RANGERS!

Major League BASEBALL begins!

Dallas Blooms FLOWER festival is really pretty.

CHICKS

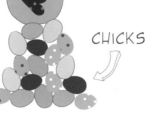

EASTER BASKET

JELLY BEANS

CHOCOLATE EGGS

LANTERNS

On EASTER SUNDAY, we go to church, have egg hunts, and enjoy an Easter parade.

The KOREAN Festival of Lanterns celebrates Buddha's birthday.

It's FIESTA San Antonio!

HELLO!
HOLA!

BYE!
ADIŌS!

YES!
SÍ!

We speak both SPANISH and English at home.

On EARTH DAY, we learn how to be green.

On ARBOR DAY, we plant a new tree in our school yard.

SANDWICHES
PIZZA
FRUIT
HOT DOGS
CORN DOGS
JUICE BOX

We either take a LUNCHBOX to school, or eat in the cafeteria.

It's EEYORE'S Birthday!

21ST

SAN JACINTO Day

May

THE FIFTH OF MAY!

5TH

Cinco de Mayo is so COLORFUL!

On RAINY days, we watch T.V. or play computer games.

MEMORIAL Day

TACOS

PASTA

PIZZA

FRIED OKRA

KIMCHI

CHICKEN FRIED STEAK

STEAK

RIBS RICE AND BEANS

On MOTHER'S DAY, we treat Mom to a buffet lunch after church.

We have SUPPER around the family table.

THE EAGLE HAS LANDED!

The Johnson Space Center in Houston has the world's largest display of MOON ROCKS!

Our class goes on a field trip to THE ALAMO.

It's warming up. We get outdoors and go SWIMMING, or play football or field hockey.

Dolphins and whales play in the water off the GULF COAST.

JELLY BEANS   CARAMELS   HARD CANDY   CHOCOLATE BARS

We love CANDY!

LOLLIPOPS

STEE-RIKE!

LITTLE LEAGUE is the best.

June

It's SUMMER!

It's CHILDREN'S DAY. We celebrate just being a *kid*.

1ST

WOOHOO!

We have our Summer Break.
Almost THREE MONTHS off school!

We wear COWBOY BOOTS
to the local dance hall.

FISHING

KAYAKING

ROCK CLIMBING

GOLD PANNING

Some of us go to summer CAMPS.

Gray foxes, mule deers, and
prairie dogs ROAM FREE on the hills.

The Texas **LONGHORN** has horns wider than my dad is tall!

Mom teaches us how to make **BUNDT CAKE**, brownies, and cookies.

Texas **FOLKLIFE** Festival

On **FLAG DAY**, the Stars and Stripes flies high.

14TH

Emancipation Day is also called **JUNETEENTH**.

19TH

On **FATHER'S DAY**, we love to spoil our dad.

SOCKS

POWER TOOLS

AFTERSHAVE

BARBECUE EQUIPMENT

We spend the weekend at a **DUDE RANCH**.

July

MY NAME IS ALEXIS ...

The **PAGEANT** season begins.

We wear our very best to church on SUNDAYS.

RAMADAN also falls in other months.

LEMONADE

BLUE RASPBERRY

RAINBOW

COLA

We eat POPSICLES in the sunshine.

GOD BLESS AMERICA!

4TH

INDEPENDENCE Day

TUBING down the Comal River is awesome!

We just love our COUNTRY music.

Abuela makes us breakfast TACOS.

We spend the WEEKEND in the Texas Hill Country.

National LATINO Family Expo, San Antonio

DR. PEPPER

ROOT BEER

LEMONADE

CHOCOLATE MILK

Dad takes us to the local FLEA MARKET.

We cool down with our favorite DRINKS.

August

I have my very own **SADDLE**.

NEIGH!

The nights are **HOT**. It's hard to sleep.

2ND

It's **FRIENDSHIP** Day.

The **ARMADILLO** is the official small mammal of Texas.

We take the R.V. to the Gulf Coast for some **BEACH** time.

TIME TO SET A SPELL.

We love to **SWIM** in summer.

12TH

It's International **YOUTH DAY**.

Mamá grows NATIVE PLANTS in our backyard.

AGAVE

BLACK-EYED SUSAN

PRICKLY PEAR CACTUS

LANTANA

ROUND AND ROUND!

STEP

START

Granny teaches us the TEXAS TWO-STEP.

27TH

Lyndon B. JOHNSON Day

DON'T MESS WITH TexaS

Our dad drives a big TRUCK.

CHICKEN

BARBECUE

SAUSAGES

BEANS

RIBS

The local CHUCK WAGON serves up a feast!

September

It's FALL. The school year begins.

HAPPY GRANDPARENTS' DAY

It's GRANDPARENTS' Day!

WORLD'S BEST COOK

On LABOR DAY, we have a backyard barbecue.

THEY'LL JUST WANT TO MOVE IN!

11TH

PATRIOT Day

National FOOTBALL League season begins!

PRETZELS

NFL ROCKS!

HAMBURGERS

CORN DOGS

HOT DOGS

SODA

TURKEY DRUMSTICKS

FRIED DOUGH

Papá says we can't feed the local WILDLIFE.

The STATE FAIR of Texas is huge!

MEXICAN Independence Day

16TH

CONSTITUTION Day

FAJITA BURGER

CHICKEN AND DUMPLINGS

BLACK FOREST CAKE

QUESO

VIETNAMESE CRAWFISH BOIL

Our favorite DISHES come from just about everywhere!

The PECAN STREET Festival begins.

We go for ICE CREAM along San Antonio's River Walk.

OctobeR

Scissor-tailed flycatchers **SOAR** over fields.

It's World **TEACHERS'** Day.

NBA! NBA!

National **BASKETBALL** season begins.

5TH

#1 TEACHER

We go on a **FIELD TRIP** to the Austin Nature and Science Center.

SO CUTE!

COLUMBUS Day

VANILLA CAKE $1.00

MUFFINS $1.50

$2.00

FRUIT COBBLER

BROWNIES 50 CENTS

COOKIES 50 CENTS

$1.50

BAKE SALE

At the local **PUMPKIN PATCH**, we pet baby animals, paint a pumpkin, and go on a hayride.

We have **BAKE SALES** at school.

GERMAN-American Day **6**TH

Abuelo makes the best **CHURROS** ever.

Mom makes lots of goodies for **BREAKFAST**.

BACON AND EGGS

WAFFLES

DONUTS

YOGURT

GRITS

BIG BEND

The **CANYONS** at Big Bend National Park are awesome!

PANCAKES

SAUSAGES AND GRAVY

Dad loves **OKTOBERFEST**.

R.I.P.

31ST

It's **HALLOWEEN**! We decorate our yards and go trick-or-treating for candy.

NOVEMBER

DAYLIGHT SAVING ends.

CLOCKS GO BACK

We gobble SAUSAGES, pretzels, and strudel at Wurstfest.

KNACKWURST

BLUTWURST

LANDJAGER

LEBERWURST

BRATWURST

11TH
VETERANS Day

NATIVE AMERICAN Heritage Month

EL DÍA DE LOS MUERTOS

I'm HOME-SCHOOLED by my mom.

On **DAY OF THE DEAD**, people leave out food and trinkets for loved ones who have passed away.

LEAVES start turning. We rake them up and jump in!

AMERICA RECYCLES Day

AWESOME!

15TH

We have a short school break for THANKSGIVING.

THANK YOU!

PECAN PIE

PUMPKIN PIE

20TH

CHILDREN'S DAY

ROAST TURKEY

CORNBREAD

POTATOES

DRESSING   CRANBERRY SAUCE

It's UNIVERSAL CHILDREN'S Day.

We spend THANKSGIVING with family and friends.

DeceMbeR

WINTER is here.

15 Opera House Rd,
Sydney, NSW
2000
301

We send Christmas GREETING CARDS to friends and family far away.

10TH

It's HUMAN RIGHTS DAY.

Mom makes a different ADVENT CALENDAR every year.

POPCORN   TINSEL

xmas decorations

LIGHTS

CANDY CANES

BAUBLES

We hang wreaths and DECORATE the tree.

It's CHRISTMAS VACATION! We go caroling and see the Christmas lights in town.

KWANZAA celebrates family, community, and culture.

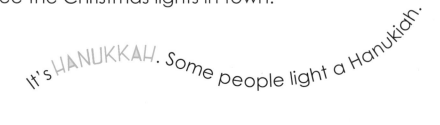
It's HANUKKAH. Some people light a Hanukiah.

We exchange gifts on **CHRISTMAS DAY**. Then it's feast time!

24TH

We hang our STOCKINGS on Christmas Eve.

25TH

CORNBREAD

COLLARD GREENS

PIE

OYSTERS AND SHRIMP

CATFISH

To celebrate **LAS POSADAS**, we devour tamales on Christmas morning.

We have a SCHOOL BREAK over Christmas and the new year.

HAM

SQUASH CASSEROLE

COOKIES

RED SNAPPER

PRÓSPERO AÑO NUEVO!

PANCHO CLAUS brings presents to kids in need.

31ST

On NEW YEAR'S EVE, we watch fireworks and make lots of noise to bring in a brand new year.

Our State

BIG FACTS

NICKNAME: Lone Star State

MOTTO: Friendship

SONG: *Texas, Our Texas*

TREE: Pecan

FLOWER: Bluebonnet

PLANT: Prickly Pear Cactus

LARGE MAMMAL: Longhorn Cattle

SMALL MAMMAL: Armor-plated Armadillo

BIRD: Mockingbird

FISH: Guadalupe Bass

INSECT: Monarch Butterfly

SHELL: Lightning Whelk

SPORT: Rodeo

DANCE: Texas Two-Step

DISH: Chili

There are 14 million cattle in our state!

Everything is BIG in Texas!

Our thanks to Texas advisors Janet Lenhart and Yitka Winn, and to the wonderful kids of Roosevelt Alexander Elementary School in Katy, Texas. Also thanks to Jen and Tony Barton, to our dedicated publisher Anouska Jones, and the whole team at Exisle. — TM + TS

First published 2016

EK Books
an imprint of Exisle Publishing Pty Ltd
'Moonrising', Narone Creek Road,
Wollombi, NSW 2325, Australia
P.O. Box 60-490, Titirangi
Auckland 0642, New Zealand
www.ekbooks.com.au

A CiP record for this book is available from the National Library of Australia

ISBN 978 1 925335 06 4

Designed and typeset by Tina Snerling
Typeset in Century Gothic, Street Cred and custom fonts
Printed in China
This book uses paper sourced under ISO 1 4001 guidelines from well-managed forests and other controlled sources.

10 9 8 7 6 5 4 3 2

Author Note

This is by no means a comprehensive listing of the events and traditions celebrated by Texas's multitude of ethnic people. The entries in this book have been chosen to reflect a range of modern lifestyles for the majority of Texan children, with a focus on traditional 'Texan' elements and themes, which are themselves a glorious mishmash of present, past, introduced and endemic culture. Content in this book has been produced in consultation with native Texan advisors, school teachers, and school children, with every intention of respecting the cultural and idiosyncratic elements of Texas and its people.